Give Me Some Space!

Give Me Some Space!

Edited by Kate Agnew

Illustrated by Garry Parsons

EGMONT

First published in Great Britain in 2003
by Egmont Books Ltd
239 Kensington High Street
London W8 6SA

ISBN 1 4052 0599 7

10 9 8 7 6 5 4 3 2 1

A CIP catalogue record for this title is available from the British Library

Typeset by Dorchester Typesetting Group Ltd
Printed and bound in Great Britain by the CPI Group

Contents

Introduction

The world of space is endlessly fascinating, exerting a peculiar hold over our imaginations. Are we ever going to know what is out there? Is there life on Mars? Could there really be a parallel universe with another planet similar to our own? Maybe we won't ever know the answers to these questions, but speculating about them provides some fantastic material for stories

Give me Some Space!

as you'll discover in this exciting collection.

Perhaps somewhere out there is a world made up of creatures a bit like people, going to school every day just like you do. Imagine being transported into a completely different universe . . . In Steve May's story, Martin, ill in bed with a temperature while his friend is struggling to explain the Big Bang in assembly, finds himself literally blown away. Assemblies will never be the same again when you've read this thrilling story.

If it's space travel that fascinates you, you'll be intrigued by the teleportation device in Douglas Hill's *The Talking Toaster*. It may look like something you'd use to prepare your breakfast, but this clever machine is no ordinary toaster: it has a secret life all of its own, or it would do, if only it could reorientate itself. In Ann

Introduction

Jungman's story Wisteria's mother prefers the traditional means of transport for a witch at Halloween – her broomstick – but Wisteria discovers that space travel is a far more thrilling prospect for a young witch. The exciting exploits of this thoroughly modern witch will have you riveted.

Linda Sargent's *Moon Pig* is, by contrast, a gentle, thought-provoking tale about the world around us. When Will looks up at the night sky the enormity of the world is hard to imagine and his own tiny place in it hard to understand. This touching story blends ordinary, everyday human existence with all the myriad possibilities space has to offer. If you've ever looked at the stars and wondered how it all came to be you'll be fascinated by Linda Newbery's *Starry*, which shows a whole new world opening up to Allie when she starts to think about

Give me Some Space!

how this world began. It's almost impossible
to imagine a time before the Big Bang,
and while Allie is wondering about the
planet big changes are happening in her
own life.

In Pippa Goodhart's story Mrs Johnson
tries to explain to her class the science of
growing plants. She is adamant that plants
need sunlight to grow, but when Meera
takes her own tiny seed home and drenches
it in moonlight something quite miraculous
begins to happen. Pippa Goodhart brings
science and magic together in a
memorable tale.

Whether you like your stories full of
dramatic adventure, exciting scientific
ideas, or intriguing possibilities to mull
over, there is sure to be something in this
special collection that you will enjoy.

Kate Agnew

The Talking Toaster

—

DOUGLAS HILL

Jess woke up, yawned, and peered down at Roxy, her cat. As usual, Roxy was lying by her feet, but he wasn't sleeping. With his head up, he was staring past her.

Turning, Jess saw a toaster on her bedside table. At least, it looked like a toaster – a square box, made of shiny metal, with an opening on top. But it seemed very out of place, sitting there

Give Me Some Space!

between her lamp and her radio.

'Where did that come from?' Jess wondered aloud.

'Myow,' Roxy said, staring.

Roxy was a black cat, except for a white patch on his chest, and he was a very curious cat too. Jess's mum often said that Jess and Roxy were alike – both young, slim, dark and lively, and more adventurous than was good for them.

Jess slid out of bed, studying the toaster. She would be eleven in three weeks, but she didn't think it was an early birthday present. Why would anyone give her a toaster? And, if it was a present, why wasn't it wrapped?

Besides, she had never seen a toaster like it. It didn't seem to have a lead or a plug, the slot on the top was far too wide for a slice of bread, and its front held a lot of

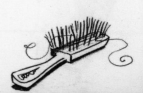

The Talking Toaster

small round dials covered in tiny squiggles.

Frowning, Jess reached towards one of
the dials.

And a snappish voice said, 'Don't
touch that!'

Jess jumped, while Roxy said, 'Yow!' and
shrank back with his ears flattened.

'Who said that?' Jess demanded,
looking around.

'I did, of course,' the voice snapped.

On the front of the toaster, two spots
above the dials began to bulge. Then a
narrow slit appeared on each bulge – and
began to *open*, like eyelids.

Inside the bulges, Jess saw small red
lights, like angry bloodshot eyes.

'Ow!' Roxy cried, the fur lifting on his
back, and Jess jumped back.

'Don't worry,' the voice snapped, 'I
couldn't harm you even if I wanted to.'

3

Give Me Some Space!

Jess circled watchfully around the strange object. Definitely no wires or anything, she thought. Yet, somehow, the voice was coming from inside it.

'Whoever,' she muttered to herself, 'would want a talking toaster?'

The red eyes glared. 'I am not a toaster!' the voice spat. 'I am a Caster, the very latest model! Somehow I have cast *myself* from my world to this backward planet, where I do *not* want to be!'

It's some kind of trick gadget, Jess thought, smiling. Probably from her dad, who liked gadgets and jokes. 'Really?' she said. 'What's a Caster?'

'I am a machine,' the voice said, 'that *sends* things from one place to another, instantly, over any distance. Even to other planets.'

4

The Talking Toaster

'Clever,' Jess said brightly. 'Sort of like emailing parcels.'

'You could say that,' the machine agreed. 'Though I send things further and faster than your email.'

Jess grinned, having thought of two things that made her certain it was a trick. 'But if you're a machine,' she said, 'how can you talk to me like a *person*? And if you're from an alien planet, how do you know my *language*?'

The voice sighed. 'I have a full robo-serve *mind*, as do all advanced machines on my world. And since I arrived here, *hours* ago, I've been using your radio to tap into broadcasts on the airwaves – learning your language, and finding out about this planet.'

Jess blinked. Those answers sounded almost believable. And the machine did look a bit alien . . .

Give Me Some Space!

'All right,' she said. 'Let's see you do it.'
She picked up a slipper. 'Let's see you send
this to . . . to the moon!'

'Don't be silly,' the machine snapped.
'How would you *see*, if I did? Anyway, I
can't send things to places I don't *know*.
Only to the 216,780,412 places that my
memory holds data on.' It paused. 'Still, I
can send things to places near me, that I
can *see*, without needing pre-set data. So . . .
give me the object.'

Jess moved forward, reaching to put her
slipper into the machine's slot. Then she
gasped when, from each end of the
machine, two spindly little arms shot out.
Small pincer hands at the ends of the arms
snatched her slipper and dropped it into the
slot. Then one of the hands touched one of
the dials.

The slipper vanished – and reappeared,

at once, on a chair across the room.

'Eyow!' said Roxy.

Jess's eyes went wide. Then she laughed excitedly. 'It's *true!*' she cried.

'At last,' the machine grumbled. 'Now, perhaps . . .'

'Let's do it again!' Jess interrupted. 'Let's send something to . . . the bottom of the garden!' Her gaze fell on Roxy.

'Nyow!' Roxy said, backing away.

'No,' the machine said. 'I'm more concerned about finding a way to get home.'

'Finding?' Jess repeated. 'Don't you *know* how?'

'Not exactly,' the machine said.

Jess was shocked. 'Even though you have a super mind that can learn a language in minutes, and remember millions of places?'

'The fact is,' the machine said glumly, 'I

7

can't get home because I don't know how I got *here*. I was on my special shelf, chatting to a robo-cleaner who was polishing the floor – and then, suddenly, I was here. It's a total mystery.'

'Did your workings go wrong somehow?' Jess wondered.

'Certainly not!' the machine snapped. 'Robo-serve machines *never* go wrong!'

'But *something* must have happened,' Jess insisted. 'Maybe you've forgotten.'

'I don't forget!' the machine spat. 'My memory is *perfect*!'

'But here you are,' Jess murmured.

'Yes,' the machine said unhappily.

'Maybe some of our scientists could help,' Jess said. 'I should tell my dad . . .'

'No!' the machine said quickly. 'Your scientists will wreck me, trying to learn how I work. *No one* must know about

8

me. But *you* could help . . .'

'Me?' Jess asked, startled. 'What could
I do?'

'Bring me data,' the machine told her.
'Books, perhaps, with pictures of the
Galaxy that might show my home star. If I
could work out where it is from here . . .'

But then another voice broke in. It was
her mum's voice, from downstairs.

'Jessica! Breakfast! Hurry up, or you'll be
late for school *again*.'

'I have to go,' Jess said quickly. 'But I'll
get some books.'

'Thank you,' the machine said.

The eyes and arms slid back into the
machine, while Jess rushed around getting
dressed and ready for school. But at the
door she paused. 'By the way, I'm Jess.
What's your name?'

'I am a robo-serve *machine*,' the voice

9

said, 'not a child or a pet. My users just call me Caster.'

Jess smiled. 'Then I'll call you . . . *Cas!*' And she rushed away, nearly tripping over Roxy who was also hurrying towards breakfast.

She went through the day as if lost in a dream, annoying her teachers and puzzling her friends. All she could think about was the machine, Cas, and its – *his* – problem. But no matter how she pondered, she couldn't think what to do or how to help.

At least she remembered to visit the school library, where she took out three books about space. And when school ended she raced home, wondering if Cas might have already found a way to leave.

But he was still on her table, grumbling about being bored after hours of tapping into daytime radio. Bringing out his eyes

and arms again, he scanned the books in a few seconds – finding nothing of use.

'Perhaps you could get me next to one of your computers, Jess,' he said. 'I might tap into your World Wide Web to see what I can find.'

'We have a computer downstairs,' Jess said. 'I could sneak you down during the night . . .' She paused. 'Cas, have you had any more ideas about how you got here? Can you remember anything more about what happened?'

'Only what I told you,' Cas said. 'I was on my shelf, talking to the robo-cleaner – then I had a strange feeling, like *flying* – and I found myself here.'

'Flying?' Jess repeated. 'You didn't mention that before.'

'It was very brief,' Cas said. 'Probably the movement from there to here.'

11

Give Me Some Space!

Just then, Roxy arrived. Purring, he leaped onto the table, twisting and turning as Jess stroked him, bumping against Cas.

The bump made Cas rock slightly and slide an inch or two towards the table's edge. And, for Jess, a light dawned.

'Cas!' she cried. 'When you felt you were flying, could you have been *falling*? Maybe that robo-cleaner knocked you off your shelf! And the fall could have moved your dials or something!'

'I doubt it,' Cas said. 'I would remember that.'

'Not if the fall hurt your memory and made you forget,' Jess said.

'I told you, I *never* forget,' Cas snapped. 'My memory is *fine*. See for yourself.'

His arms appeared, opening his front panel just below the dials. Inside, Jess saw a floating cluster of tiny triangles, hundreds

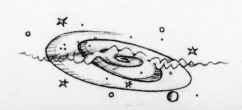

of them — each the size of a pinhead, all sparkling brightly.

'Raow,' Roxy said, blinking.

'That's my memory,' Cas said. 'Every triangle holds half-a-million units of data.'

'Brilliant,' Jess breathed. 'What are all the dark triangles on the right?'

'That's spare memory,' Cas said. 'Not yet needed.'

'And the little patch of dark triangles on the left?' Jess asked.

'What do you mean?' Cas demanded. 'There *are* no dark ones on the left.'

'There are,' Jess said, pointing.

Cas's eyes bulged and stretched further, like elastic, until he was able to peer into his own insides. He stared silently for a moment, then his eyes drew back to their normal place.

'Jess, I apologise. You were right.' He

Give Me Some Space!

sounded shaken. 'My fall must have jolted that bit of my memory loose, and I didn't know because I can't access that bit while it's loose. So robo-serve machines *can* go wrong . . .'

Jess patted his cool metal. 'You didn't go wrong, Cas, you had an accident. Can you fix it?'

'I have no microtools,' Cas said sadly. 'There's not supposed to be any *need* to repair robo-serve machines . . .'

Jess frowned. 'I could try something my Dad used to do to fix the picture on our old TV. It might knock that bit back into place – but it *could* make things worse.'

'If there's a chance,' Cas urged, '*try*!'

'Right,' Jess said.

Holding Cas with one hand, she slammed her other hand against his left side, with an echoing crash.

The Talking Toaster

'Waow!' Roxy said, leaping from the table as Cas bounced and skidded. Then Cas closed his eyes and went silent again.

'Cas?' Jess said anxiously. 'Are you all right?'

But the silence went on.

'Cas!' Jess said. 'Say something! Did I make it worse?'

'Jess . . .' Cas said softly. And then his eyes popped out again, glowing. 'Jess, it worked!' he said. 'I remember everything! The robo-cleaner knocked me off my shelf – and the fall shifted my dials, which threw me out into space and brought me here. But now I know just how to set my dials to cast myself back!'

Jess drooped. 'So you'll leave?'

'Of course,' Cas said.

'Can't you stay a little longer?' Jess pleaded.

15 *

Give Me Some Space!

'Jess,' Cas said gently, 'I know I've been lucky – that fall could have thrown me anywhere in the universe, but it sent me to you. You've been very kind and I'll never forget you, but I'm a Caster, with work to do on my own world. We must say goodbye.'

His hands flickered over his dials with dazzling speed. At once, his shape began to grow misty and the slot on top stretched wider while the rest of him squeezed smaller – as if he was somehow turning inside out.

Then, without any sound at all, he was gone.

'Wow,' Roxy said softly.

Jess sighed, blinking back a tear. Then she picked Roxy up and cuddled him.

'I think,' she whispered, 'I'll be a space scientist when I grow up. I'll build a

The Talking Toaster

wonderful spaceship, so that we can go and visit Cas. What about that, Roxy?'

'Mrow,' Roxy said, not sounding very sure about it at all.

Moon Pig

—

LINDA SARGENT

'Photos you said?' Will's mum was peering into the fridge.

'Not in there,' teased his dad who was standing at the back door staring up at the sky, as usual.

Will looked up from his book, 'S'OK,' he said, 'I won't need them until Tuesday. Mrs Goddard only comes in on Tuesdays.'

His mum came and sat at the table,

stirring milk into her coffee. 'She's doing family history with you, is that right?'

'Yeah, it's brilliant,' Will said, 'next week she's going to show us how to search and stuff on the computer.'

An odd glance slid between his mum and dad then, as if they had said something without actually speaking.

'Well, Saturday today, so no school and no work!' Will's dad stretched. 'Any volunteers for a bit of allotment-clearing later?'

'I'll help,' Will said. He enjoyed digging, getting rid of grass and weeds ready for next spring's planting. His dad had even given him his own patch of ground and he could grow anything he wanted on it, as long as it wasn't weeds.

'And I'll come down later,' his mum said. 'If you like?'

19

Give Me Some Space!

'All help gratefully received,' Will's dad laughed. 'Seen my wellies anyone?'

'You'd better change into your old jeans too,' Will's mum told him. 'That mud down there's a special sort, if you ask me.'

'Alien mud?' his dad said, googling his eyes. It was one of his favourite jokes – anything awkward or hard to explain must be from another planet.

'Quite likely,' Will's mum agreed. 'Something round here's alien anyway.' She got up and started stacking up the breakfast things.

Coming back downstairs from his room, Will heard his mum and dad still in the kitchen talking. He was just about to go in when he realised that they were talking about him.

'Better tell him soon,' his dad was saying.

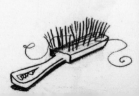

Moon Pig

'Otherwise it's going to be tricky. I
mean, how are we going to explain about
the photos?'

'You're right,' his mum agreed, 'we
should tell him where he came from – him
and Moon Pig.' She laughed then. 'You and
your aliens, I don't know.'

Will felt his cheeks heat up and then
his whole body. Aliens? What did his
mum mean, and how was it connected
to him and the photos? He didn't
understand. And Moon Pig – his silver
mascot pig that he'd had since he was
a baby, this was something to do with
her too. Weird! It had been his dad
who had named her Moon Pig. He
said it was because she was special
and one day he'd tell Will why. But he
never had.

★　　★　　★

ιirs in his room, Will examined
ιn the mirror. Sludgy brown hair
ιreckles. He didn't *look* like an alien!
Still, he wasn't really sure what an alien
would look like. He screwed up his eyes.
They were strange now that he looked at
them. That green colour was definitely
odd, not like Mum's or Dad's. Yet he didn't
feel like someone – something – from
another planet.

'Oh, there you are!' His mum made him
jump, he hadn't heard her come up.

'Sorry,' he mumbled, wondering if his
voice was the voice of an alien, but it
sounded just the same to him, only quieter.

'You all right, love?' His mum came
across and put her hand on his shoulder.
He shook it off.

'Come on,' she said, 'Dad's waiting and
you need to put your wellies on too.'

Moon Pig

★   ★   ★

All that day, Will became quieter and
quieter, only speaking if he was spoken to,
even when his mum said, 'Hey Will, it's
your birthday next Saturday! Eight, eh?
How will that feel, I wonder?' He just
kept on digging, telling himself that
they were just pretending to treat him
normally when all along they knew he was
different. Not one of them. It wasn't fair.
Anyway, what did an alien want with
birthdays? It was hard to imagine what
sort of presents he'd get. Nothing felt right
any more.

And even though his dad made his
amazing cheese and fried potato supper
that night, Will wouldn't eat it.

   'Perhaps you're getting a bug,' his mum
said, feeling his forehead. 'Hmm, you do

seem a bit warm. I'll take your temperature later, just in case.'

Must be the green blood, Will nearly blurted out, but not talking had got to be a habit now and so he just nodded.

He could hardly wait to get upstairs. It was where he felt safe. 'I'll be up to take your temperature, Will, OK?' his mum called after him.

'Didn't even want to play Super Dog on the computer tonight,' he heard his dad saying. 'Must be sickening for something.'

'A little on the high side,' his mum announced as she checked his temperature. 'How are you feeling?'

'OK,' Will grunted, pulling his duvet up round his neck. He just wanted her go and leave him alone.

She sat for a minute, blowing at his

24

Moon Pig

planet mobile, making it go round and trying to get him to look. He knew. But he wasn't playing. Eventually she got up and went towards the door.

'I'll look in on you later. All right?' She sighed and dimmed the light right down to its usual blue-green glow. Starlight, it was called. Now Will knew why.

As soon as she'd gone, he was out of bed. He opened the top drawer of his desk and took out Moon Pig. She was really no bigger than his thumb, but it was easy to see her expression. She was smiling, he could tell. A contented pig, comfortable sort of grin was marked out on her tiny face. She glowed like a piece of moonlight. Will took her over to the window. It had been a while since he'd looked at her; it had started to feel babyish playing with a miniature silver pig.

Give Me Some Space!

'Moon Pig,' he whispered to her. He knelt on the window ledge and stared out into the shadow-smudged garden.

The moon was up – a bit more than half-full. He knew about the phases and had marked them out on a chart on his bedroom wall. His dad had told him all about the planets and pointed out the constellations. They sometimes looked at the moon through his dad's binoculars.

It seemed different now though.

'Moon Pig,' he whispered again. He held her up. Down in the meadow, an owl called eerie and wild through the soft night dark.

'Moon Pig,' Will held her close to his face. Clouds straggled across the moon and he wondered, 'Is that where you're from? Is that where I'm from? Am I the only one?' he asked her, shivering and afraid. But men had landed there and no one had

reported seeing any aliens. The moon was
lifeless, everyone knew that. And yet . . .

Will rested his head against the cool
glass and held Moon Pig in his hand,
cradled tight. He stared and stared at the
hard glitter of stars and the ghost-faced
moon. The more he stared, the faster the
great dark loneliness of space seemed to
rush at him, sucking him far out to where
aliens belonged.

He gripped his fingers, but he realised his
hand was now empty. 'Moon Pig?' He
mustn't lose her! 'Moon Pig?'

'Yes?' the girl standing next to him
answered. She was tall, almost a grown-up,
and had green, green eyes.

'You're Moon Pig?' he asked. And there
was just the sliver of a nod in reply as she
took hold of his hand. She was very slim

27

Give Me Some Space!

and pretty as pigs go. In fact, she was very unpig-like. Except for her grin. When she smiled, Will knew.

'Where are we?' he asked. Looking down, he saw the grey dust covering his toes and the craggy silent landscape stretching away into the everlasting dark. 'The moon? We must be on the moon!'

She didn't answer, instead she pointed out to space. 'Beautiful, isn't it?'

Will rubbed his eyes and looked again. 'The Earth,' he said softly. 'It's so blue.'

'It's your home,' said the girl, still grinning at him.

'So blue,' he repeated, 'in all that blackness. It's like something magic.'

'It's where you live, where we live,' the Moon Pig girl said once more, still pointing. As she pointed, she let go of his hand and Will could feel himself being

Moon Pig

lifted up high above the moon's surface.

Soon he started falling and falling, crashing through the star-specked darkness of space towards the Earth. And as he fell, the Earth seemed to be rolling towards him like a giant shiny blue marble, with white clouds covering huge splashes of sea, and the brown land in between. He saw the fires of wandering nomads glowing in the deserts. There were great masses of light too from the cities. All that life, he thought, all those people. People like me! This is my home, where I belong. Where we belong, me and Moon Pig.

Will began cartwheeling, faster and faster. He clamped his eyes shut. Such a long way. He opened his mouth and started to scream. When his dad came in, he couldn't tell him why.

*   *   *

Give Me Some Space!

'Poor old you,' his mum said next morning, 'falling out of bed like that – must have been a bad dream. Do you want to tell us about it?'

Will looked up from his toast. 'P'raps,' he said.

His dad passed the marmalade across the table. 'It was a good scream,' he said. 'You must have been practising secretly.' He smiled and made Will think of Moon Pig. 'I found her outside in the garden this morning, by the way,' his dad added and handed Moon Pig to him. 'Right under your window, covered in a sort of grey dust.'

With Moon Pig in his hand again, Will started talking and talking. Out it all came; the whole alien worry, the dream thing, how it was scary but not scary. How real it had seemed.

His mum and dad listened very quietly

and then, finally, his mum said, 'We've got
something to tell you, Will.'

He listened.

'Well, what do you think?' his dad asked
when they'd both finished, each having put
in their own bit of the story about really
wanting a baby and not being able to have
one of their own and how they chose him,
Will, over all the others they could have had.

'Will?' his mum was frowning.

'Amazing,' he answered, shaking his
head, 'you chose me?'

His mum and dad nodded hard,
smiling now.

'Wow!' Will said. Questions stirred
around in his mind. 'Is that why you got
funny about the photos and stuff?'

'Yes,' his mum said. 'We didn't want to lie
to you and send you off to school with you

31

not knowing that, although everyone in the family is your family, oh dear . . .'

'I don't actually look like them?' Will put in.

'But that doesn't matter,' his dad said, 'it is probably for the best anyway!' He pulled one of his gruesome faces.

'And Moon Pig?' Will asked. 'She's got something to do with all this, hasn't she?'

That glance again between his mum and dad, but this time he knew what it meant.

'Your mother sent it to us to give to you, when we first had you,' Will's mum told him.

'There's a photo of her too,' his dad explained, 'and some other things. Do you want to have a look?'

'Yes. Yes, please,' Will said after a moment, suddenly knowing that she would have green, green eyes.

Moon Pig

There was a lot to think about. It was good to know he wasn't an alien after all. Well, he was in some ways, but it felt all right. Exciting and special. He couldn't wait to tell people!

On Saturday, when Will opened his present from his mum and dad, there was something else amazing.

'A telescope,' he said, looking at them both, 'a real telescope.'

'Now you can have a proper look at the moon,' his dad told him. 'Find the place where the first men actually landed.'

'Yes,' Will said, 'now I can.'

He put his hand in his pocket and felt the familiar smooth silveryness of Moon Pig, knowing that she would be grinning.

Wisteria and the Witch's Rocket

ANN JUNGMAN

Wisteria was cross — she was very, very cross. Her mum had gone off with all the other witches and had refused to take her daughter with her.

'You can come next Halloween, when you're older,' she had said as she tucked Wisteria up in bed.

'Not fair,' grumbled Wisteria to herself, as she crept out of bed and downstairs.

Wisteria and the Witch's Rocket

Peeping round the door, Wisteria saw her
father glued to the Internet.

'Good,' muttered Wisteria and slipped
out of the back door and tiptoed down the
garden to the shed. Quietly, she opened the
shed door and looked inside. Only one
broom was left, a very large broom indeed.

'Left you behind too, did they?' asked the
broom crossly. 'A fine way to treat a witch
and a broom on Halloween, I must say.'

'Why did they leave you behind?'
demanded Wisteria.

'You may well ask,' grumbled the
broom. 'They left me behind because I am
too old.'

'And they left me because I am
too young.'

'Why don't we go for a lovely ride
together?' suggested the broom. 'That will
show them.'

Give Me Some Space!

'Promise to get me back here before Mum returns?'

'No problem,' the broom assured her, 'easy peasy. Now you just get me out of this corner, young lady, and we can be off and away.'

So Wisteria dragged the broom outside and climbed onto it and, suddenly, she was flying high, high, high in the air. It was wonderful and Wisteria shrieked with joy. The broom flew round and round the trees, up over rooftops and, after a while, began to play with the stars.

'Can we go back now please?' asked Wisteria, who was beginning to get a bit cold in her pyjamas and dressing-gown.

'Certainly not,' yelled the broom, 'I'm having far too much fun. How do you fancy flying up and over the moon?'

'No!' yelled Wisteria. 'It's far too far and

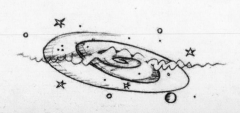

it's too cold. I want to go home.'

'Tough,' cried the broom. 'Here we go.'
Wisteria closed her eyes as they sailed
over the moon.

'We made it,' shouted the broom. 'I knew
I could do it,' and he did a somersault
while Wisteria held on desperately.

Looking up, Wisteria saw a rocket
hurtling towards them. 'Look out,'
screamed Wisteria.

But it was too late, they flew straight
into the rocket. For a moment nothing
happened, and then Wisteria found herself
looking into the kindly face of an alien
hanging from a ladder.

'Oh dear, oh dear,' said the alien. 'What
a good thing we caught you, you might
have got your death of cold up here.
Broom, whatever were you thinking of
coming up so high?'

37

Give Me Some Space!

'Felt like it,' grumbled the broom. 'Wanted to explore.'

'Not with a little human witch person on your back, that was very naughty indeed,' said the alien shaking his head. 'Now, come on both of you, into the spaceship and get warm.'

Wisteria and the broom were hauled into the spaceship, where ten aliens sat looking at them. 'Well, don't just sit there gawping,' said the first alien. 'Go and get blankets and hot soup. Can't you see she's blue with the cold?'

Soon, both Wisteria and the broom were wrapped in nice warm silver space blankets and Wisteria was eating the most delicious soup ever.

'I'm Commander Placibus, commander of this spaceship in the service of the planet Bongoloid,' explained the alien who had

rescued them. 'This is my crew.'

Wisteria smiled and the crew all smiled and waved back.

'What I don't understand,' said Wisteria, 'is how you all speak English.'

'Oh, we don't speak English, we speak Bongoloid,' they all assured her. 'We are surprised that you speak such good Bongoloid.'

'English must be the same as Bongoloid,' said Wisteria smiling. 'Isn't that lucky?'

'Indeed it is. Now, young lady, we want to know what you are doing so far from home.'

'It is Halloween, and I wanted to go for a ride with my mother, who is a witch, but she said I was too young.'

'Yes,' nodded the aliens.

'So I slipped out and went to the garden shed where the brooms are kept.'

Give Me Some Space!

'Yes,' agreed the broom. 'And she got lucky because I was there and, out of the kindness of my big heart, I decided to give the little lady the ride she wanted.'

'Did you want to sail up to the stars and over the moon?' asked Commander Placibus.

'Oh no,' wept Wisteria, 'I only wanted to go over a few rooftops and then back home before Mum gets back.'

'That's right, blame me for everything,' grumbled the broom. 'All I wanted was a bit of fun and I end up the baddy. Well, I've got my side of the story to tell too.'

'Put him in the broom cupboard,' shouted the commander. 'He talks too much.'

'I've got my rights,' yelled the broom, as the aliens dragged him off to the broom cupboard. Commander Placibus locked the

40

Wisteria and the Witch's Rocket

door. 'Now you just cool off in there,'
he told the broom, who kept banging on
the door.

'So, my dear, what we need to do is
find your family on our computers.'
Suddenly a panel appeared with
hundreds of computers on it. 'Now give us
your address.'

'22, Avon Gardens, Little Doggleswick,
England.'

'Got it,' cried one of the aliens. 'Come
here Wisteria. Is this your father?' Wisteria
looked at the screen and there he was, still
lost in the Internet.

'That's him,' said Wisteria. 'And he's still
working away on his computer. That
means my mum's not home yet.' She burst
into tears.

The aliens all gathered round and patted
her and looked very worried.

Give Me Some Space!

'If my mum gets home and finds I'm not there, she'll be so angry and worried,' wept Wisteria.

'We'll get you back there in no time,' said Commander Placibus. 'So dry your eyes and we'll go and sort out that silly broom.'

One of the aliens opened the broom cupboard and called out, 'Alright broom, you can come out now.' The broom ambled out, looking very happy.

'We want you to take Wisteria back to her house as quickly as possible,' Commander Placibus told him, 'and no messing about.'

'Oh, I'm not going back to Earth,' the broom told him. 'No way. I have fallen in love with your very charming Bongoloid broom in there and I've decided to stay here.'

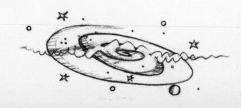

Wisteria and the Witch's Rocket

'Only if you take Wisteria back to Earth safely first,' said Commander Placibus.

'Oh, you won't catch me that way,' laughed the broom. 'Once I've left here, you'll never let me back to be with my own true love. Oh no, you can forget it.'

Wisteria started to howl. 'I'll have to stay here forever and ever, just because of that horrid broom.'

'Who was it who wanted to go out on her own?' asked the broom. 'You can't blame me for everything.'

'I've got it,' shouted Commander Placibus. 'I know what we'll do, we'll build a tiny rocket for Wisteria to ride instead of a broom.'

'Oh yes,' smiled the aliens. 'Much better than a broomstick and much more reliable.'

So all the Bongoloid engineers set to work to create a Wisteria-sized rocket to

get her back to Earth. Wisteria watched, fascinated, as a beautiful blue rocket with silver stars popped out of a machine and landed at her feet.

'Oh it's lovely,' cried Wisteria, 'so much smarter than that old broom.'

'You just watch your language out there,' came a voice from the broom cupboard.

Everyone laughed, then Commander Placibus cried, 'To work. All we need to do is get an exact reading of where your garden is in Doggleswick and then we can direct you back.'

'No problem there, Commander,' said the chief engineer. 'It's all programmed and ready to go.'

'And my dad is still working on the computer and my mum isn't home yet,' giggled Wisteria.

Wisteria and the Witch's Rocket

'With a bit of luck, they need never know you went to the wrong side of the moon and ended up in a Bongoloid rocket,' smiled Commander Placibus. 'Now, put on this little suit for warmth.'

Wisteria put on the silver suit they handed her and she gave all the aliens a big hug. 'My mum will wonder what happened to the broom,' said Wisteria.

'You can just tell her I'm doing very well for myself,' yelled the broom from the cupboard. 'And good riddance.'

'Ignore him,' said the commander, 'and just remember, you'll be the most modern witch in the world, the only one who rides on a rocket rather than a broomstick. Now, off you go.'

'Thank you so much,' said Wisteria, 'I shall miss you all.'

'Don't worry, we'll come and visit now

Give Me Some Space!

we know where to find you,' cried the aliens. 'Bye Wisteria, byee.'

And Wisteria flew off sitting astride her rocket, towards Earth. 'Byee,' she called. 'Thanks so much, this is the best fun. Much better than a broomstick.'

Wisteria landed quietly in her garden. Silently, she took off her space suit and carefully hid it in the shed with the rocket. Then she tiptoed up to bed. Dad was still working at the computer.

Wisteria lay in bed thinking about her great adventure. Then she heard her mum come in.

'Any trouble with Wisteria?' she asked.

'Not a peep,' said Dad.

Wisteria smiled to herself and looked forward to the time when she could go out with her mother and fly on her lovely rocket.

46

Wisteria and the Witch's Rocket

'I'm so glad I'm the most modern witch in the world,' she smiled to herself as she fell asleep.

Moonflower

—

PIPPA GOODHART

Meera's body sat at the table in the
classroom with the other children, but her
mind was floating up into the sky outside.
She chewed on her pen and gazed out of
the window at the moon shining pale in
the morning sky. It looked, thought
Meera, like a chappati, round and dimpled.
If you didn't know better, you'd think that
the moon was as flat as a chappati too.

Moonflower

Things weren't always as they seemed.

'Perhaps Meera can tell us?' Mrs Johnson's sharp voice made Meera jump. 'Moonbeaming again, Meera? Or can you tell us what conditions a plant needs in order to grow?'

'Er . . .' Meera looked to her twin, sitting two tables away, but Seema wasn't offering any help. Meera thought about the pots growing herbs on the windowsill at home. Mum sometimes got her to water them.

'They need water,' said Meera.

'Good,' said Mrs Johnson. 'What else?'

'Um, I suppose they need soil too, or they'd fall over.'

'Water and soil and . . . ?' Every face in the classroom was looking at her now, and Meera's brain went blank. She blushed and looked away. Mrs Johnson sighed. Meera knew she was thinking, 'I never have this

Give Me Some Space!

trouble with Seema.' Some people said it out loud, but Meera knew that lots more people thought it.

Meera and Seema were the same on the outside but, on the inside, one was a good girl and the other was 'difficult'. Seema was the good girl. She did what she was told, promptly and neatly and well. Meera didn't. Meera found the conversations she could have in her mind with herself were nearly always more interesting than what teachers and parents and even friends told her. So she moonbeamed, escaping into her mind and away from the classroom, or kitchen, or wherever she was at the time. It made teachers cross. Mrs Johnson scowled.

'Can anybody help Meera with the answer?' Yes, they all could. Arms shot up all around.

'Sunlight. Plants need sunlight!'

Moonflower

'That's right,' said Mrs Johnson. 'And now, I'm going to let you all have a go at growing a plant. We will have a little competition to see who can grow the tallest sunflower and we'll experiment by giving each of the plants slightly different conditions to see exactly what suits them best.'

Mrs Johnson looked down her nose at Meera, then smiled to the rest of the class. 'I expect that Meera will grow hers without giving it any sunlight at all!' They all laughed, all looking at Meera, but this time Meera tossed her dark plait over her shoulder, crossed her arms and glared back.

'As a matter of fact,' she said. 'I will!'

'Oh, indeed?' said Mrs Johnson. 'And do you think you have a chance of winning?'

51

Give Me Some Space!

'I might!' said Meera. Seema rolled her eyes to show what she thought of that, and she laughed with the others.

Mrs Johnson gave out the seeds next morning. Seema had brought some of Gran's fruitcake to mix with soil for hers. 'It should make the seeds grow fast,' she told Meera. 'Remember how Gran said that her cake is nourishing with all those raisins in it? Some of the boys are watering theirs with apple juice and orange juice. And Katie's putting a bit of chocolate near hers because she thinks the smell will make the plant want to grow out of the soil to reach it. That'd work on me! Have you decided what to do with yours yet, Meera?'

'I told you yesterday,' said Meera. 'I'm growing mine without sunlight.'

Moonflower

'Not really? But it won't grow, you know, not without any light. Mrs Johnson said so.'

'I never said it wasn't going to have any light,' said Meera. Then she turned away and wouldn't say any more. But she could feel Seema watching her as she put soil into the plastic flowerpot, pushed in a slim, stripy seed, and watered it from a jamjar. Then she covered the pot with a bag she'd made out of black paper to keep it dark.

'Line the pots up on the windowsill,' said Mrs Johnson. 'Make sure that your name is clearly marked.'

'But mine mustn't have any sunlight,' said Meera.

'Well, if you're going to insist on this silliness, then you'd better put yours into the stock cupboard. But I think we all

know what the result of this is going to be,'
sighed Mrs Johnson.

'Can I take it with me when it's
going-home time, please?' asked Meera.

'Whatever for?'

'Part of my experiment,' said Meera.

'Oh, if you must, Meera,' said
Mrs Johnson.

Seema tried to walk home beside Meera.

'Why are you taking your pot home?'
she asked. 'You're being really stupid, you
know? Everybody thinks so. Why don't you
grow it properly in the light like everybody
else? That's what Mrs Johnson wants you
to do.'

But Meera marched on, holding her
covered pot in front of her, and she
didn't answer.

★　　★　　★

54

Moonflower

Meera and Seema went to bed at their normal time, but Meera didn't go to sleep. She lay on top of her hairbrush to make sure that she was too uncomfortable for that. She waited and listened to the sounds of Seema's breathing becoming slow and sleepy. She heard her parents going to bed, heard her little brother going downstairs for a glass of water, and then stillness, marked by the tick-tock of the clock on her bedside table. Meera watched the curtains and, finally, just after midnight, they began to glow with light as the moonshine reached them.

Silently, Meera pushed back her covers and then the curtains. She took the black cover off her seed in a pot and sat the pot on the windowsill in a stream of silvery moonlight.

Give Me Some Space!

'There's your light, little seed,' she whispered. 'Now, get growing and show Seema and the others that you can beat them all!'

She knelt at the window, her head propped on her hands, and she gazed out at the big silvery-blue moon and thought of the men who had stood on the moon and bounced around and stuck in a flag and then gone home. She thought to herself, I bet their teachers told them it was stupid to think they or anyone could ever stand on the moon.

The moon moved across the sky as Meera watched and thought. When the moonlight went from the window, Meera shaded her pot and got back into bed. But her mind kept thinking about what seemed impossible but might just be possible as she warmed to sleep.

Moonflower

$\star \quad \star \quad \star$

Next morning, the children looked at the bare soil in their plant pots. 'It'll be a few days before there'll be anything to see,' said Mrs Johnson. Yet that evening, when Meera uncovered her pot in the moonlight, there was already something green poking through the soil in her pot. Meera threw her plait over her shoulder and smiled as she put it in the moonlight once more.

Over the next few nights, Meera watched for moonlight and uncovered her growing young plant to moonbathe in the light each night.

'Why do you keep yawning?' asked Seema at school. 'Mrs Johnson's been giving you funny looks.' But Meera didn't tell. Night after night, she kept herself awake while Seema slept and watched as

her little plant grew, a bit like somebody sitting up in bed, stretching sleepy arms, and turning to see the moonlight coming in through the window. The green spike of life grew upward, spreading wide two fresh green leaves.

Meera knew that the other children were muttering things and laughing at her at school, but she didn't care. She found a bamboo cane in the garden shed and pushed that into the soil and carefully tied her plant to it with soft wool to try and keep it strong and tall. Seema watched as the black paper hood over the pot in their bedroom was replaced by taller and taller hoods. She didn't ask Meera questions about it any more. And she'd given up even watering her own seed in a pot after it began to go fluffy with mould. 'Mine's not going to work,' she told Meera.

Moonflower

Then, one moonlight night, Meera's
plant bloomed into flower. It unfurled a
broad speckled silver-gold circle fringed
with narrow silvery-white petals.

'I'm taking it to school today,' Meera
told Seema next morning. 'Would you like
to see it before the others?' Seema nodded.
So, with their bedroom curtains holding
back the sunlight, Meera took the hood off
her plant.

'Oh!' said Seema, and her hands fluttered
to her mouth. Then she looked at Meera.
'But it isn't a sunflower, is it?'

'No,' said Meera. 'It's a moonflower,
grown in moonlight. That's why
it's different.'

Seema touched the flower very gently.
'It's beautiful,' she said.

Seema carried Meera's bag so that
Meera could carry the tall plant to school.

Give Me Some Space!

Meera put the pot on her table and put her hand up.

'Meera, yes?' said Mrs Johnson.

'My plant's got a flower,' said Meera. Everyone went quiet and turned to look at her.

'Already?' said Mrs Johnson, glancing at the row of pots on the windowsill where a few tiny shoots were showing but not anywhere near big enough to flower. 'That's rather surprising when your plant hasn't had any sunlight to help it grow.'

There were a few tittering laughs around the class.

'It's had moonlight,' said Meera.

'Oh,' said Mrs Johnson, 'I see. Well, perhaps you'd better show it to us.'

So Meera lifted the black hood from her plant and there were gasps and then silence

all around as, for just a moment or two, the silver-white flower shone luminously, before its brightness dulled and the flower began to wilt as they watched. Nobody said anything, then Mrs Johnson snorted a kind of laugh.

'Well, I must admit that I've never seen anything quite like that before, Meera, but I am quite sure that no plant can grow without sunlight. You look in any book on the subject and you'll see that I'm right.'

'Books don't know everything,' said Meera. Mrs Johnson went pink.

'They know a great deal more than any cheeky little girl does! And I feel quite sure that if I look in a book of garden weeds, I shall find a fast-growing scraggly plant with a big grey flower and that you, Meera, have planted one of those in your

61

pot and tried to trick us all. I don't believe
for a moment that you've been up catching
the moonlight and growing your seed that
way! You'd better throw that horrid plant
in the bin!'

The plant had lost its beauty as Mrs
Johnson talked, wilting in the sunlight and
the scorn, and Meera seemed to have
wilted too. But suddenly Seema was on
her feet.

'You're wrong, Mrs Johnson,' she
said. 'Meera has done it properly. I've
seen her in the night when she thought
I was asleep. It's a real moonflower,
grown from the seed you gave her and
it should win the prize!' Mrs Johnson
blinked rapidly.

'The prize is for the tallest sunflower,
Seema. It is not for moonflowers. Now,
Meera, throw that thing away and

62

Moonflower

then I want you all to take out your
maths books.'

The moonflower plant had wizened as
they watched, and its petals had fallen.
Meera slowly tipped it, pot and plant, into
the bin. Then she glanced at Mrs Johnson
who was busy writing on the board. Meera
bent down and quickly took something
back out of the bin; something that she
held tight in a fist. She sat down beside
Seema. As the others took out their maths
books, Meera uncurled her fist to show
Seema four slim, stripy silver things in the
palm of her hand. 'Seeds,' she said.

'Can I help with them?'
whispered Seema.

Mrs Johnson frowned at Seema. 'I want
quiet, please!'

But Seema took no notice. She was
looking at Meera who smiled and nodded,

Give Me Some Space!

'We'll grow them together.'

Then they both tossed back their plaits and gazed out of the window and wondered about the moon and space and whatever was beyond, while Mrs Johnson talked about fractions.

Space Assembly

—

STEVE MAY

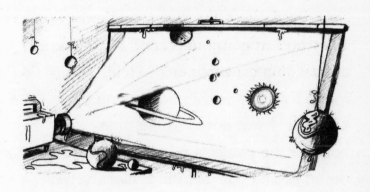

You can run but you can't hide: the further you go the nearer you get.

Heidi is on the stage in the school hall. She's raging mad. She's got a projector and a CD player and lots of posters and pictures. She's furiously shuffling and stacking things.

'Hi Hei, what's up?' asks Rosie Watchett.

'I'm doing space for assembly. I've got

Give Me Some Space!

music and pictures and poems and facts.'
'Sounds cool, what's the trouble?'
'Trouble is, the Universe is missing!'

No way I'm going to school. I'm supposed
to be doing assembly, with Heidi, about
space. I'm supposed to be making the
Universe. I was going to use ping-pong
balls for the planets and tennis balls for
the stars, and put them in a black velvet
bag. Then, when the time came for the
Big Bang, they were all going to go
flying everywhere. But I haven't got
anything ready. So here I am, in bed,
playing sick.

Hotter and hotter and hotter.

'It's a bad case of the flu,' Dr Baker says.
'Best sweat it out.'

I'm shivering and sweltering. The quilt
feels hot and heavy.

Space Assembly

'I've got to do assembly today,' I croak.
'It's about space travel.'

'No way, pal,' says Dr Baker.
'You're grounded.'

And then it clicks with me – I am sick!
No pretending.

I feel as though I'm looking at Dr Baker
through the wrong end of a telescope. She's
miles away, floating out of the door. The
telescope is all glass, and there's a silver
block rising up the middle, rising and rising
and rising.

And suddenly – oh no! Dr Baker's
shrinking and morphing, and her hair's
gone red and she's turned into Heidi. Heidi
is screaming at me.

'Martin King – where's my Universe!
Where's my Universe! You good-for-nothing
waste of space!'

But she can't get me because I'm lifting

off, ever so slowly. Lifting off like a rocket, lifting away from her, so she's getting tinier and tinier.

Heidi is alone on the stage. The hall is hushed. She nods and Mr Traynor switches on the CD player. Spooky music seeps out, electronic twangs and gushes. The lights dim. The projector glares on a huge white screen and Heidi clears her throat.

'We live on the Earth. Earth is here.'

She points with her pointer. A photo of the Earth taken from space flashes up on the screen: white clouds, blue sea, green and brown land.

'The Earth is a planet, which moves around the Sun.'

An image of the Sun flashes onto the screen, and the Earth picture shrinks and shrinks until you can hardly see it. Heidi's pointer clacks on the screen.

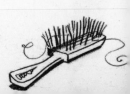

Space Assembly

'The Sun is a star, just like the millions of stars you see in the sky at night.'

'Why are they so small then?' sneers Piggy Brasswick.

'Because they're so far away,' replies Heidi.

On the screen, the Sun starts to shrink, and hundreds of other stars flash up around it.

'Stars gather together in groups called galaxies. Our Galaxy is called the Milky Way.'

'How about the Dairy Milk?' shouts Piggy Brasswick. 'Or the Turkish Delight!'

Heidi whacks her pointer on the floor. 'They are chocolate bars, we're talking serious space, and you are messing up my assembly.'

Piggy shrinks in his seat.

Heidi speaks again, in a loud whisper. 'Our Earth is small, the Sun is huge, but compared to the whole Galaxy, the Sun is tiny, and compared to the whole Universe, our Galaxy is tiny too.'

'How tiny?' demands Piggy.

Give Me Some Space!

'As tiny as a pea in our playground.'

On the screen, little flashes start to whizz backwards and forwards.

'Everything in the Universe is made of the same things. You, me, the trees, the rocks, the earth, the stars . . .'

'Even Mr Traynor?' shouts Piggy.

'Yes, even Mr Traynor. We're all made of tiny, tiny, tiny little things called particles, so small you can't see them, even with a microscope . . .'

'Hey, pal, you are hot.'

This fuzzy guy is sitting on a cloud. He's round but vague. The silver block's still rising but I'm clinging on. The fuzzy guy floats up with me. He's pulsing like a flame in a draught.

'If you get much hotter,' he says, 'you are going to melt.'

'How would you know?'

Space Assembly

'Oh, I'm a particle, called Vector Boson. I've seen it all before.'

I don't answer because the silver block is rising faster and faster. It's gushing up like a wave in a tide and I'm surfing. Faster, faster, headlong. But not upwards, it's like I'm spreading in all directions, like milk in tea.

Fuzzy Vector Boson guy is travelling along beside me. He flies for a split second, then disappears, then pops back up again.

'Hey,' he laughs, 'you have melted.'

'What's the next stage?'

'You'll go gaseous.'

There's a pop, like your ears pop when you go up a hill in a car, but it's all of me that's popped. I'm going faster and faster, whirling round like a flock of birds in the sky.

Vector Boson is flickering on and off,

puffing and stretching. 'Hey, I can hardly keep up. And if you get any hotter . . .'

But I must be getting hotter because suddenly there's another pop, and now I'm streaming luminous like a flame stretched through the nozzle of a vacuum cleaner. Boson's last words are echoing in my head. 'If you get any hotter, you'll turn into light.'

On the screen, the camera is plunging forward through stars and planets, and particles and moons.

'Hey,' calls Piggy, 'this is making me feel sick.'

Heidi ignores him. 'There's no doubt that the Universe is huge,' she says. 'But one question needs to be answered. Is our Universe finite or infinite?'

'What does that mean?' shouts Piggy Brasswick.

72

Space Assembly

'If it's "finite", that means it's got an end. It's closed, it's got boundaries, you could walk all round it if you ever had enough time. "Infinite" means it goes on for ever and ever and ever and ever, and no matter how far you walked or ran or flew in a rocket, you'd never come to the end.'

'So? Who cares?' shouts Piggy Brasswick.

'Well,' said Heidi, 'if it goes on for ever and ever and ever, there must be multiverses.'

Mr Traynor cleared his throat. 'What are multiverses?'

'They are other versions of our world.'

'Other versions just like us?'

'Yes and no. Some will be exactly like us, but others will be different.'

'Different how?'

'Well, if the Universe goes on for ever and ever, then every thing that can possibly happen, must happen somewhere, sometime, right?' Heidi

73

Give Me Some Space!

glances round. 'So in another Universe somewhere, Mr Traynor isn't a teacher, he's a superstar in a boy band.'

Mr Traynor blushes. 'I did once think of a career in show business.'

Piggy shouts out, 'Does that mean I'm really still in bed at home?'

'In some universes, yes,' replied Heidi.

'And I wish this was one of them,' added Mr Traynor.

Now I am flying. I'm like a snooker ball, all tight and hard and cased up, and I'm shivering. A kind of regular shudder runs through me right from the inside.

'How long can this go on?'

'Forever or a blink.' It's Boson again, puffing to keep up.

'How did you get here?'

'I smacked into another particle, but now

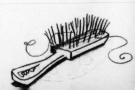

Space Assembly

I'm only virtual so really I'm not here at all.'

'Where am I going?'

'To the edge of the Universe, if you don't hit anything first!'

Heidi nodded to Mr Traynor, and a picture of a clock flashed up on the screen.

'Once, before time began, all the suns and stars and particles and everything were packed together into a space smaller than a single flake of dandruff on Mr Traynor's collar.'

A spotlight flashed on, and glared down at an empty spot on the stage.

'At this point,' explained Heidi, 'we were going to experience the Big Bang at the start of the Universe, but Martin King's got a cold.'

The glow looms up huge, like it's all round me.

'What's going on?'

Give Me Some Space!

'Don't worry,' says Boson. 'We're getting near the Big Bang.'

'Didn't that happen a long time ago?'

'Sort of. But it's also always happening, one for every universe.'

The glow flared again, like a balloon, and the next thing I know, we're inside it! I'm tumbling down, in a curve, but I'm going so slow it's like I'm standing still.

'You're being sucked into a black hole at the creation of the Universe.'

'What's that way ahead there stretching into the distance?'

'That's your nose. As we approach the centre of the black hole, space stretches out to infinity, and time slows down.'

Piggy Brasswick cupped his hands to his fat lips and made a booing sound. Everyone else joined in.

Space Assembly

'You'll just have to imagine the Big Bang,' snarled Heidi.

'That's right,' said Mr Traynor, standing up.

But the booing and jeering got louder and louder.

Heidi turned on the CD player and music blared out, like howling cats and whooshes.

'That is enough . . .' began Mr Traynor, but stopped with his mouth open.

'This is it,' drawled Boson, every word taking three days to say. By now my brain is so far from my ears, I forget what he says before I hear it.

'That means we're nearly . . .'

The school hall is lit up in a flash of white light. The flash is so bright and so white, even the dirty green walls shine like white fire and Piggy Brasswick glows like an angel on a Christmas

77

Give Me Some Space!

*tree. Whooshing through the fire in every
direction, there are streaks of gold, silver, purple,
blue, hissing and criss-crossing.*

*Everyone gasps, and in the space of that gasp,
it's all over.*

Suddenly, there's a rip and a snap like
twanging elastic and I'm back to normal
size and powering out the other side of the
black hole at the speed of light.

'We're out the other side,' gasps Boson,
'at the start of another universe.'

'Wow,' I say, 'I wonder what it'll be like?'

*The hall is quiet again, except for some faint
snortings and slurpings.*

*'So there could be millions or trillions of
universes, all different or similar or the same,'
Heidi concluded.*

'Very interesting,' murmured Mr Traynor, 'but

Space Assembly

I don't think there could ever be another school like this one. Now it's time for first lesson,' he added, wiping away the slime from his beak with a tentacle.

And the youngsters, very impressed by Heidi's assembly, slithered and squirmed out of the huge palace of shells with only the faintest swish and slap of their suckers.

Starry

—

LINDA NEWBERY

Allie usually liked staying with Nan and
Grandad, but this time she hadn't wanted
to come. Nothing was ever going to be
quite the same again, and she wanted
things to stay just as they'd always been.

Nan had forgotten to put the wheelie-bin
out. She trundled it round to the front, and
came back inside, puffing at how cold it

was. 'It's a starry, starry night out there!' she told Allie. 'Shall we put our coats on and have a proper look? Scarves and hats and gloves too, it's so cold.'

When they went outside, Allie could see that there was already frost on the garage roof, and the grass felt crunchy under her shoes. She looked straight up, looked and looked, and felt dizzy. So many stars! On and on and on they went, deeper and deeper, farther and farther away. The sky and the stars made her think of a Christmas decoration, sparklier and spanglier than any she had ever seen.

'What's sky?' she asked Nan, and her breath made a misty cloud in front of her. She breathed some more, just to see it.

Nan thought for a moment. 'Well, it's air. But that's the bit just above us, the bit we

81

can see in daytime. Higher than that, well, it's – it's nothing.'

'Nothing? But how can it be nothing when it's got all those stars in it? What happens when there's no more nothing – what's after that?'

'More nothing, Allie love.' Nan tucked Allie's scarf more warmly round her neck. 'It goes on for ever.'

For ever! Allie tried to imagine that. As far as she could think, then even more. And more after that! Never reaching an end, never becoming anything that wasn't nothing. Tilting her head back to see, she felt dizzy, and clutched at Nan's hand. It felt funny holding someone's hand when you both had knitted gloves on.

'Why don't we fall off?' she asked, imagining herself and Nan whirling and whirling into all that blackness, not

82

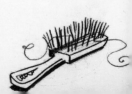

knowing which way was up.

'Allie, you and your questions – I wish I knew half the answers!' Nan said laughing. 'But I do know the answer to that one. It's the Earth, you see. It wants you. It won't let you fall off. So it pulls you to it like a magnet.'

'Like the magnets you've got on your fridge?' Allie already knew about gravity, but it was fun getting Nan to explain.

'Sort of. It pulls you to the ground and holds you there.'

Allie lifted her feet, one after the other. 'I can't feel the pull.'

'Ah, but you can. Jump up, both feet at once, and what happens? See? It pulls you straight back down. It doesn't want to let you go.'

'But supposing it stopped pulling, just for a minute?'

83

Give Me Some Space!

'I don't think we need worry. I've been walking around for fifty-something years, and it's never stopped pulling yet. Come on, love – we'll be frozen to the spot if we stand here any longer. Bedtime for you.'

But Allie wasn't tired yet; her head was aswirl, full of stars that wheeled and danced and winked. She had a last, long look at the endlessly-sequinned sky.

It was warm and bright inside, and Grandad was sitting at the computer. Allie pulled off her coat and scarf and went over. 'Are you on the Internet?' she asked. 'Look up "space"! Look up "stars"! I want to know how the world began, and *all* the worlds.'

'Big subject for a small girl,' Grandad said, but he started clicking his mouse and searching.

'Into your pyjamas, anyway,' Nan said.

84

Starry

'The Universe can wait while you get ready for bed. I'll make cocoa.'

Cocoa was one of the nice things at Nan's house; they didn't have it at home. Allie wondered what Mum and Dad were doing and why they hadn't phoned back. Wasn't there any news? But when she came down, Grandad had found a good website. He showed her pictures — of the craters of the Moon, of a Sun that swirled like a Catherine wheel on firework night. Then he showed her a moving picture that started on Earth and moved farther and farther out into space, leaving the Moon and Sun and Galaxy behind, on and on into the dizzying depths of nothing.

'But it's not nothing,' Allie said, standing behind Grandad and leaning on his shoulder. 'It's fuller than full.'

'Did you know,' said Grandad, 'there are

two hundred billion stars in the Milky Way Galaxy? And that's only the nearest galaxy to us.'

'A billion is a million times a million.' Allie knew that from school. 'I'd never be able to count that far.'

'I shouldn't think you'd even want to try. And here's something else I've found out – the Earth, our Earth, is twelve billion years old. Twelve billion! That's an awful lot of birthdays.'

'But where was the Earth before it was born?' Allie asked. 'Where did it come from?'

'Allie, you're asking hard questions again.' Nan brought the cocoa. 'Come on, drink this up while it's nice and hot.'

Grandad clicked the mouse. The giddy star-flow disappeared, and instead he found a whole page of print. He peered closely at

the screen while Allie sipped her drink.

'Where did the Earth come from?'
Grandad said. 'Well, let's see. There are
things here about Big Bangs and black
holes, and the whole Universe starting from
the tiniest, tiniest point you could imagine.
Think of that! All starting tiny and getting
bigger and bigger, growing and stretching
all the time.'

Allie tried to make her cocoa last a long,
long time, but Nan noticed. 'Bed for you,
young lass! Or it'll be tomorrow before we
know where we are.'

Soon Allie was in bed and dreaming. She
was standing outside again, looking at the
sky, when the Earth stopped pulling and
she floated above the rooftops, above the
tallest trees, up and up. At first, the Sun was
warm on her face but, as the air cooled,

87

Give Me Some Space!

she was glad she'd put on her warm scarf
and gloves. The scarf's tasselled ends
fluttered into her face as she soared. She
looked down at Earth as it grew tinier and
tinier – a blue-green sphere, bright as a
Christmas tree bauble, with the cold silver
Moon in attendance. She saw the Sun and
the other planets, she saw whirling moons,
she saw shooting stars with tails of red.
Suns and stars, some so faint they were
only misty blurs, some so huge that she
thought they'd swallow her up in a
golden blaze.

Forgetting which way was up, she turned
somersault and tumbled, falling and falling,
through sky and space, till she landed
gently in Nan and Grandad's spare bed
and saw that it was morning. Something
inside her gave a jump of excitement when
she remembered what day it was. Looking

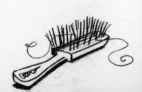

Starry

out of the window, she saw the grass all silvered with frost, but the trees and the shed and the fence looked firmly anchored to the ground, exactly the same as usual.

'I had such a weird dream,' she told Nan and Grandad downstairs. 'I saw the Earth from out in space, and it was tiny. So tiny, I wondered how there was room for all of us.'

Nan was sitting at the computer. 'It's tiny but it's huge,' she said. 'Now, see what you think of this!'

Allie looked. Nan clicked the mouse, and brought up a new screen-saver – black, full of stars, that moved away from you and sucked you into the deepest deeps of dark.

'Just like my dream!' said Allie. 'Only we're so far out that we can't even see the Earth. It's still there though.'

'I certainly hope so,' Nan agreed.

89

Give Me Some Space!

'Breakfast?' said Grandad. 'Cornflakes? Weetabix? Porridge?'

'Ooh, porridge I think,' said Nan, 'on such a cold morning.'

Allie was still thinking about her dream, and how tiny the Earth had looked, shrinking and shrinking as she moved out into space. 'The funny thing is,' she said, 'I know the Earth is a tiny speck of dust compared to space, and we're even tinier specks of dust to fit on it. But I don't feel tiny inside my own head. I'm tiny *and* enormous – I'm ti-normous!'

'Inside your own head is the best place to be,' said Grandad, clattering saucepans in the kitchen. 'It's the only place you know where you are.'

'I think, therefore I *am*.' Nan shut down the computer. 'That's what some philosopher said. We are getting into deep

thoughts this morning, aren't we?'

The phone rang while they were eating their porridge. Allie knew from Nan saying, 'Oh! Oh! How lovely!' what must have happened. And as soon as she put the phone down, she came over to Allie and hugged her. 'You've got a new little sister! Born just an hour ago. Everything's fine, your dad said. And she can't wait to see *you*. Soon as we've finished, we'll go to the hospital and see them all.'

'An hour old!' Allie said, wondering at it. 'And I *wanted* a sister. Has she got a name?'

'Not yet,' said Nan.

'Isn't it funny,' Allie said, 'that we say "an hour *old*", when she's nearly as young as she could be?'

'Eat up your porridge, lovey,' said Nan, 'and then we'll get ready and go. We'll need to scrape the frost off the car.'

Give Me Some Space!

Ten minutes later, Allie was standing exactly where she had stood last night with Nan, gazing up at the stars. Now the sky was fresh and blue above rooftops glistening with frost. But she knew the stars were still there. They didn't go away.

When she had first heard that Mum was going to have a baby, Allie hadn't liked the thought at all. Nothing would ever be the same again! But now she thought, nothing's ever going to be the same again! And it was so *exciting*.

This was her sister's birthday – her Birth Day. This day would be a special day, a birthday, every year from now on. Allie knew where babies came from – they started as tiny seeds, so tiny you couldn't see them, and they grew and grew, like the Universe. How odd that something so

enormous and something so tiny should start in the same way!

'When do babies turn into people?' she asked.

'Oh, we're off on the questions again, are we?' Nan fastened the top button of Allie's coat. 'That's another hard one. When they're born, or *before* they're born? I haven't got the answer to that one.'

'She could so easily not have been, my sister,' Allie said, 'but now she *is*. She's here. She's inside her own head!'

Grandad was scraping the side mirrors. 'I know. A little miracle, that's what she is.'

'A miracle?' said Allie.

'That's right. Because there are two hundred billion stars in the Milky Way,' said Nan, opening the back door for her, 'but there's only one of your little sister.

93

Give Me Some Space!

And only one Allie. In you get, Allie the one-and-only.'

And Allie climbed into the back of the car, snuggling into her coat, full of wonder. She was about to say 'hello' to a new person. Someone so small that she hadn't even existed this time last year; someone big enough to change all their lives.

'It's because we're ti-normous,' she said. 'All of us.'

A Family Like Mine

Question:

What do you get when you cross a spitfire
and a ballet dancer with a Christmas runaway,
a familiar face from the past, two terrapins,
four goldfish and a woman who makes
strange goat noises?

Answer:

You get a brilliant collection of stories about
the remarkable ups and downs of family life.

Would You Believe It?

Question:

What do you get when you cross a horse-backed ghost and a Dream Maker with a girl made of stone, too many baked beans, an invisible sister and a tiny figurine with needle-sharp fangs?

Answer:

You get a brilliant collection of stories about the allure of magic and mystery.

What's Cool About School

Question:

What do you get when you cross
a multi-coloured woollen worm,
a comical pencil and a hairless bear
with Aladdin's basket, a space-craft tree
and the world's biggest cucumber?

Answer:

You get a brilliant collection of stories
about the fun and the frights of school.